TO

Tony

Brief Instant

Fantasy
And
Speculation.

A collection of what ifs, might have been, and still could be poems from the beginning Big Bang to the Dark, starless Universe projected by modern science.

Throw in a bit of Fantasy to vary the mix, stir and brew, and, hopefully, an interesting read.

Hope so.

This is a collection of previously unpublished poems.

Comments and emails welcome.

Check out my Author Page on Amazon.

Contents

Unobserved
Brief Instant
Big Bang Day
Uncreation
Cosmos
Winter Ballad
Bliss
Dimensions
System Analyst
Eternities
devastation
Eyes Of Hope
Whimsy
Half Submerged And Waiting
Summer Ball
Star Gazing Live
soma
Sleeping Watch
Random Factor
Renewal
Excerpt
Exodus
Global Warming
Distress
Unobserved
Dreams And Devastation
Withdrawal – Part of the Faerie Saga
Top Moor Top
Those Black Dog Days
Communication
Diplomacy
Virus
vampire ii
Warlock
Imminent Rebirth Faeries

Void
Disintegration
eternity
eternally
ephemera
Turmoil
taste
Paralysed
Pilgrimage
Jester
Invasion
Invasion – preparation
Joshua
Rites
Evolution 1
Winter's Solstice
Overload
Not quite dreaming
Night Things
Nemesis
Shaman
Shadow Play
Moonshine
Mission Exploratory
Miscreant
The Universal Wisher Man
Alone?

Unobserved

In the beginning the Universe
Was dark, but not empty,
Full of dark matter and
Tendrils of the Cosmic Web,
Spreading out, and, where
Overlapping, birthing stars,
Blue, fast burning giants
Collapsing and imploding
To release the material to
Build a more static universe,
Birthing the God Stars,
Predecessors of stars of today
For the blink of an eye,
By space time standards
Sentient beings worshipped,
Observed, studied and speculated
Before slipping into extinction
As it expanded, galaxies crashing
And merging as they rush apart.
All matter being finite as slowly
But inevitably stars progress
Collapse. and die
Until darkness descends and
Maybe, the process will restar
And, in time, unobserved
The Gods Stars will rule again
From dark matter
And tendrils of Cosmic Webb
In a new beginning

Brief Instant

With the James Webb telescope,
Out there in the dark of space,
In its precisely calculated and
Designated observation place
Professors says there's a chance
That, in time, it just might
Capture a picture of
That first emitted light,
Travelled over billions of years
From the Big Bang of creation,
Which may present us
With the situation
That, as light travels
Faster than sound,
James Webb may,
If still around,
Capture and record
The blast of noise
Of that instant of creation,
The Big Bang's voice.
I think, rather, it will go unheard
From out there in deepest space
Thanks to the self destructive
Tendencies of the Human Race,
As a new dominant species
Fights to gain and hold sway
On the Blue Planet as it
Travels serenely on it way.
And the Universe expands,
Stars implode to lose their light
And continue their creation of
That darkest of darkest night.
For the briefest of brief times
In its violent evolving history
Our sentient species tried to
Understand its every mystery.

Big Bang Day

All was observed with interest
As they readied their new tools
Then when their Accelerator started
The Creator rewrote all the rules

Uncreation

As the Lungs of the World
Blaze away in the Amazon,
Glacial melt bleeds
Ever faster into the seas
And extinctions speed
Uncontrollably along,
Worldwide
The privileged still amass
Their power and wealth,
Squabble over etiquette
While feeding nonsense
To the masses,.
Cavernous eyes
Of starving children peer
From television screens,
But not in my backyard,
And the Earth slips
Ever closer to being
Made uninhabitable,
Our mote of dust
Drifting along in the
Endlessness of time
And space
We have indeed created
A truly Godless world

Cosmos

They stride the world
As the Master Race,
Vainly talk of their
Conquering Space.
The Earth Twitches
The Earth shakes
Volcanoes erupt
As the Earth quakes.
Ice bergs melt
Avalanche slide
Tsunami flow
Planet wide.
Pandemics rage as
Nature moves on
The Master race
Now almost gone.
Pushed back to basics
Will they survive
Do they still have
That vital drive.
In spite of assumptions
Of their own worthThey were only lice
On the face of the Earth
Just a speck of duft
Almost lost
In the vastness of
Expanding Cosmos.

Winter Ballad

The one who controls the wind
As a cushion for her feet
Drifted the dead dry leaves
Before her on the street
Playfully lifted
A lock of her hair
Caressed her cheek
With tender care
Helped her along with
A following breeze
Sang her a song through
Rustling boughed trees
Escorted her unseen to
Her Lover's embrace
Then silently turned
To leave that place
Turned to face the wide sea
And with a despairing wail
Whipped up that ocean
With a tempestuous gale
Worked out his rage
With one last desparate cry
Culminating with one
Last accepting sigh
Lashed the waves
Against the shore
The let peace
Reign once more
Never looked for her again
Just breathed one icy breeze
Causing the town one
Early unseasonal freeze
Causing she and her lover
To snuggle up in a tight embrace
As his goodbye breath icily
Kissed cool her face
Then the one who controls the wind

That lovelorn one
Resolutely turned its back
And silently moved on.

Bliss

I feel the touch
As she makes me bleed
Stroked her hair
As I let her feed
Both lying there
In such bliss
The erotic heights
Of that vampire kiss
She takes with care
She lets me live
So she can share
What I freely give
For a finite time
Though this feels so right
Now more and more I feel
The call of the night
Now I sleep
Most of the day
A lethargy that just
Won't go away
I know one night soon
She will slake her thirst
One life's last passionate night
Followed by new life's very first
She tells of the ecstasy
That by and by
Will be ours
As we fly
Unfettered and free
As of natural right
So long as we stay
Confined to night
Her lips withdraw
And now we will play
Until just before dawn
She slips silently away
And I must arise

Exercise all my will
To keep this body fit
To prolong the thrill
Prolong the time
I can enjoy the bliss
Of feeding my love
In our vampire kiss

Dimensions

Reaching through dimensions
Trying to make a being think
Something to home in on
Help this being make the link
So it can find
An active mind
Test capacity carefully
So as not to overload
Start to build the pathway
That will soon become a road
Lay the sign carefully
For the kin to read
Come assuage your hunger
Here there be feed
Slowly drain
That brain
Making the most
Of that host
As the ever needed search
Continues its reach
Through the dimensions
To find the next breach
To move relentlessly on
Before we are found
Betrayed by those mindless
Beings wandering around
Proof to all who can read
And learn too late for fear
The kin have been feeding
But are no longer here
Reaching through dimensions
Trying to make a being think
Something to home in on
Help this being make the link,

System Analyst

I am the being who walks through walls
The shadow not quite on your stair
You can never really see or be sure
That I am or am not really there
I walk those narrow corridors squeezed
Between those differing world and ages
Sweeping up anomalies, systems needing
Tuning, checking programmed stages
To keep the multiverse's progress
Within the parameters loosely set.
Many think they have seen me
But none have caught me yet.
My contract is to eternity
And all that I can ask
Is that I be allowed
To carry out my task.
They think they can catch me
As I bend time and space
Instantaneously between
Every existant place.
There is always a silent leakage
As I pass from host to host
The tell tale patch of coldness
Said to indicate the Ghost.
I have to move so quickly
I don't think I could fix
The resulting chaos caused
By letting two worlds mix.
I close each door a quickly
Make sure each is docked
Before moving through
To complete the interlock.
I find space time anomalies
Which I promptly heal and close
Once a world of dinosaurs
Passed through one of those
The programmes wouldn't let me

Quickly bend enough hyperspace
So they left intriguing puzzles
In that other parallel place.
I am the being who walks through walls
The shadow not quite on your stair
You can never really see or be sure
That I am or am not really there.

Eternities

Is the advance of science
A pursuit of the inexplicable,
An attempt at a Comprehension
Of a level which we are incapable.
Will there be a final tick of
The cosmic clock at the end
As the Star Eaters finish their meal,
Darkest of darkness descend,
And Space at last becomes
A truly empty void
Of nothingness,
Barren and devoid?
Will the once Black Holes
And the Dark Matter
Suddenly, by their time scales,
Suddenly burst and shatter
In a searing flash of recreation
Tearing through time and space
To be observed millennia later
By a recent evolved sentient race.
Grappling with their creation myth?
Or, will nothingness stretch on and on
That magnificence that had once been
Finally, irrevocably devolved and gone,
An incident in an eternity of eternities,
We, just for a while, irrelevant observers?

devastation

following my past footsteps
down through the long hall
up the winding staircase
to a door hidden in the wall
that magic door
I will never find
unless I approach it
in a right frame of mind
for it to slide open
to that magical place
outside of dimensions
outside time and space
where past present future
interweave join merge meld
so all possibilities of existence
are displayed and briefly held
before different possibilities
are newly arrayed
making redundant
those previously displayed
then my room spins wildly
and I am outside on the stair
not even sure that I
was ever anywhere
my head is throbbing wildly
sickness and nausea the cost
and my room of possibilities
which may be nonexistent is lost
and I wonder will I ever achieve
that state to see once more
the shimmering outlines
of my maybe nonexistent door
and I retrace my past footsteps
down and through the long hall
my despair heightened as I see
only spare and unmarked brick wall

Eyes Of Hope

I was in my own state
Of personal hell,
Like being trapped
In a bottomless well,
Held in a mental
Deep dark place
Until i met the woman
With the old young face
And a pair of sparkling eyes
That held me entranced,
Even hypnotised
Pulling me into
A field of green
The lushest grass
That I've ever seen
And we are running
Hand in hand
Just for joy
Across that land.
No need for rush
No place to go
Just happily running
To and fro
Until in time we reached a gate
Where no gate really should be
And she pushed me through
And those her eyes set me free
To a different world
A hopeful one
And my deep despair
Was suddenly gone.
And she of the young old face
Was suddenly blind
The price she paid
For cleaning my mind.
A sacrifice

She made for me.
Now I am whole
And I am free

Whimsy

Stringing skeins of moonbeams
Then hanging them to dry
To make a fine necklace
In the by and by

Threading them with sunrays
Ready for the time to try
To make a fine necklace
In the by and by

Add a grain or two of pure stardust
So very pleasant to the eye
To make a fine necklace
In the by and by

A necklace for my true love
Just no other reason why
To make a fine necklace
In the by and by

Half Submerged And Waiting

When half the world is half submerged
Which, on a cosmic scale, won't be long
Will the hard core of change deniers
Finally admit they really got it wrong.
For what ever cause or reason
The climate is quickly changing
What ever the cause the effect
Looks likely to be far ranging.

Like a plague of Locusts
From Africa we deployed
Developed and spread
Pillaged and destroyed:
In thanks to the planet
That gave us birth
We tipped the balance
On the beneficent Earth.

Still a planet of beauty
And, as time moved on,
A place of a different beauty
Once we are finally gone,
Maybe half submerged in water,
The Poles again covered in trees,
Maybe waiting once again for
Life to emerge from nurturing seas.

Summer Ball

They said it was a Wizard's ball
Witches attending as well
I attended out of duty
And she enticed me with her spell

We danced the light fantastic
Her perfume such a heady brew
She played witch to my wizard
As in passion we glid and flew
Two souls enjoined and soaring
Into that azure blue blue night
Dancing and whirling and suddenly
She was gone from my very sight
And only her perfume
Hanging in still air
Was any type of proof
That she was ever there

They said it was a Wizard's ball
Witches attending as well
I attended out of duty
And she enticed me with her spell

Star Gazing Live

There are seventeen billion planets
That's what astronomers now say
There are seventeen billion planets
And that's just in our own Milky Way.
Is god still in his heaven,
Now maybe in deepest space,
For surely there is other life:
We can't still be the only place.

Each planet earth like
As far as they can tell
Our instruments and distances
Don't let us see them very well.
Maybe just maybe
A few host life
Maybe just maybe
The phenomenon is rife.

Perhaps there is reason in distance
For at our present travel rate
There is no way that we can reach
For us to contaminate.
In time we may mature
Learn wisdom, understanding, grace
Maybe there will be a brotherhood
In which we can take a place.

Until then we can only wonder
And let our instruments speak
Until they confirm or not
Whether we are a unique.
With seventeen billion planets,
In other galaxies maybe more
We have time to learn humility
As we plan to evaluate and explore.

soma

the time of instant gratification
by drugs tailored for the mind
ersatz sex for the impotent
psychedelic vision for the blind
any mountain could be climbed
any bloodless battle fought
using the little needled pads
to mould and form the thoughts

and for the anti social few
the old criminal class
chemically induced obedience
in prisons walled of glass
to be open for inspection
available for all to see
in this open of open societies
where to conform was to be free

a chemical castration that
could be reversed if and when
situations demanded that
the proles should breed again
so through a glass ceiling
secure in their role
in the interest of stability
and subjugation of the prole

the meritocracy ruled
without the judas kiss
of mind controlling drugs
and chemically produced bliss
in a world of peace and comfort
a world without any war
thanks to the mighty chemical
old gods not needed anymore

Sleeping Watch

I have been here now
For more than sixty years
I know all their foibles
Understand their fears
I even mated locally
With so many great joys
We even manufactured
My two beloved boys
Which is now a problem
I'll feel so mean
When they discover
I am alien and green
We are closing the motorways
With their straight run through
To enable our landing
The only thing to do
We are the Guardians
Here to help with the rebirth
Of that battered planet
They call Mother Earth
Together we can rebuild
Hopefully restore
A healthy clean planet
For the species one more
Then maybe we can leave
And in time I can re enter
My sleeping watch
At Galactic Centre
Another crisis over
Just before too late
Maybe I'll have pleasant dreams
Of my offspring and my mate

Random Factor

Visions appearing out of dreams
The sleeper asleep
Yet neither awake
Nor really a sleep
Fashioning crystal spheres hanging
So randomly
The very randomness patterned
By the quantity
Spreading
In a velvet night
On and on
And out of sight
Into eternity
Each sphere
Sighing
Each sphere
Uniquely crying
A mish mash of tones
Crystal screams
Sounds of nightmares
Sounds of dreams
As the sleeper
Creates
Sighs
Obliterates
Crystal spheres hanging
Multiverses appear
Twinkle finitely
Disappear
Such a beauty in
Random creation
The sleeper sleeps
And sleeps on and on and on
Unaware of what has grown
Fruited decayed and instantly gone

Renewal

Shaman Queen in her feathered cloak
Reviewed the words before she spoke
Reviewed their rhythm then made start
Her voice at first low and barely heard
Then harshly strident as she stepped
The creation dance of the Sacred Bird
Traced the mating
The egg being laid
From which in time
The world was made
She danced its growth
From the birth
To that stage of
Perfect Earth
Shaman Queen danced and sang
Of that time of infestation day
That started the long but sure
Process of pollution and decay
She swung her cloak
Stamped bare feet
Sung her words
Of bittersweet
In supplication
Danced the dance
To give the world
A second chance
Fell to earth
In sleeping trance
In dreamless sleep
She could feel
The process start
For the egg to heal
Shaman Queen in her feathered cloak
Dreamed Sacred Bird rose and spoke
Danced spun paused and finally flew
Gave earth its start to slowly renew

Excerpt

Death stood at his shoulder
Overnight moved much nearer
She could see its every detail
So very much clearer

She pulled her lover to her
Beat down her need to cry
And whispered in his ear
A fond fond goodbye

He kissed her back and laughed
Said I won't be away for long
I'll miss you so my darling
Be happy while I'm gone

She watched him walk away
Cursed the gift of second sight
Knew deep in her heart
They'd not share another night

She shivered there suddenly
Felt its icy cold breath
And turning towards it
Faced her imminent death

Exodus

On the edge of the edge of nowhere
At another spiral galaxy's outer rim
Moored in a neat synchronous orbit
The fleet in formation tidy and trim.
The space elevator in construction
And they working all their worth
To turn this his virgin planet
Into a substitute green earth.

They have cruised for generations
Through the black void of space,
Searching always searching
For their new home place:
The descendants of the chosen
On their Exodus of Despair
No way of knowing now
If Old Earth is still there.

With the rising of the waters
As the temperatures got higher
The struggle to grow the food
The population would require
Caused a rising tension,
Riots and the threat of war
With the great possibility
Law would rule no more.

So they built Arks of Hope
In the orbit of the moon
Filled each huge vehicle full
With its chosen survival platoon;
To save the gene pool of the species
With the lessons all hard learned
They blasted off into the future
All bridges severed and burned.

The surviving Arks have sensed
A world of blue and green
So long has been the journey

First land for eons seen.
The sleepers have been risen
For full life to begin anew
The work is hard but rewarding
With so much to plan and do.
They have started on their mission.
The work is under way
To create another Earth
Where respect holds sway.
On the edge of the edge of nowhere
At another spiral galaxy's outer rim
Moored in a neat synchronous orbit
The fleet in formation tidy and trim.

Global Warming

Not a crisis for the Earth.
It will change and carry on
With the dominant Naked Ape
Culled, or wiped out and gone.
It's period of chaos just a pinprick
In the time of planetary existence
That changed the balance with their
Irritating growth and persistence.
Their unwritten epitaph
Brief but succinct
Once they ruled
But now extinct
With them removed
Maybe comes a time when
In the form of the bird,
The Dinosaur will rule again.
A Planetary Eden
May come to be,
Pristine and green
And pollution free.

Distress

they call him jack o' shadows
and he's never ever seen
it's only when he's gone
you know that he's been

he moves through the darkness
never in full daylight
comes into his own
only after midnight

he's that shadow down the alley
that shade of despair
though never ever seen
all know that he's there

by the cold chill in the bones
that shiver of fear
all indications that
suddenly he's near

and he lives on your discomfort
always trying to find
a person to distress
this vampire of the mind

and he feeds so very quickly
reaps emotions every one
oh so very quickly then
in a flash he's gone

they call him jack o shadows
he could be anywhere
it's only that spinal shiver
tells you that he's there

Unobserved

In the beginning the Universe
Was dark, but not empty,
Full of dark matter and
Tendrils of the Cosmic Web,
Spreading out, and, where
Overlapping, birthing stars,
Blue, fast burning giants
Collapsing and imploding
To release the material to
Build a more static universe,
Birthing the God Stars,
Predecessors of stars of today
For the blink of an eye,
By space time standards
Sentient beings worshipped,
Observed, studied and speculated
Before slipping into extinction
As it expanded, galaxies crashing
And merging as they rush apart.
All matter being finite as slowly
But inevitably stars progress
Collapse. and die
Until darkness descends and
Maybe, the process will restar
And, in time, unobserved
The Gods Stars will rule again
From dark matter
And tendrils of Cosmic Webb
In a new beginning

Dreams And Devastation

In my dreams the sky is sombre,
The earth arid and lifeless and brown
Scorched and burnt and seared
By the acid rain pouring down.
Coasts have receded
As water has taken the land
New rolling seas where
There once was dessert sand.
All from a climate change
That Nature began
But very quickly exacerbated
By the actions of man.
The lands are deserted
As man has moved on;
He has reached for the stars,
Packed his bags and gone.
There is life in the Oceans
A maternal soup where it teems
Perhaps in a hopeful ending
To my strange dreams.
Maybe in a future millennium
In a long distant when
It will burst forth
And take the land again.
A very different Earth
With maybe a very different end,
The New Life not repeating
Old Life's self destructive trend.

Withdrawal – Part of the Faerie Saga

The ships were loaded
All preparations made
The people all boarded
Now the last card played

They altered racial memory
Of those creatures left behind
Just a few subtle adjustments
To a still developing mind
Perceptions subtly shaded
So the race of Faerie Folk
Far from being warriors
Became an almost joke

Gone the fierce fighters
And in their place
Were planted images of
That much gentler race
Little flying creatures
Magical and rare
That flittered and fluttered
In and through the air

The retreat then covered
Came the time to leave
A time for looking forward
Not a time to grieve
Then Oberon and Mabs
According to plan
Took ship and left Gaia
To the ascendant race of man

Out into the Galaxy
And deep unexplored space
To find and build a New Earth
To take that Old Earth's place

Top Moor Top

There's a field of white windmills
Up there now on Top Moor Top
Whirring spinning slender sails
That just never seem to stop.
I suppose there is a certain beauty
As you look about and around
But I just can't adjust to
Their constant field of sound.
It's seems there to remind us
There always is a cost
That in the cause of progress
Old values can be lost.
I have lost my type of beauty
In this a favoured place
No matter how they turn and spin
With their statuesque grace.
A sacrifice of beauty
In the cause of Mother Earth,
Or is it just a gesture
For the profit that its worth?
Still over in the Amazon
Forest destroyed without real need
Replaced by fields of Soya bean
To make cheap animal feed.
This world is so sadly changing
And in truth my friend
I am glad I'm not at life's start
But rather nearer its final end.
I stand amongst those windmills
And the beauty that I find
Will be of unspoilt hills and moors
Stored safely in my mind.
Whirring spinning slender sails
That just never ever seem to stop.
There's a field of white windmills
Up there now on Top Moor Top

Those Black Dog Days
(Dedicated To All Who Suffer Mental Illness)

The Black Dog's on my shoulder
And he's whispering in my ear
Sowing doubt in my mind,
Filling me with fear.
I can subdue him with meds,
Quieten him most of the day,
But lethargy of the intellect
Is a high price to pay.

But the Black Dog escapes:
Somehow he always reappears
To sit on my shoulder
And to whisper in my ears.
My world is dark and gloomy
As the Black Dog takes control.
And he preaches despair
To the very core of my whole.

He is trying to tell me
How I should think
And I try to erase him
By setting down to drink;
And I get a hangover
And I'm back in despair
For my Black Dog
is still sitting there.

I need to be rid of him
I need to be free
But I think that Black Dog
Could be the death of me,
Or, smothered in drugs
To keep him at bay,
I'll just be drifting through
Blank tranquillised days.

But the Black Dog won't win
For I've learned how to fight
And one day in time I know
Things will come right.
I don't ask your pity
Just that you try understand
For me sometimes I'm living
In an foreign alien land.

Communication

There's a throbbing in the air
Carried on the breeze
Resonating slowly outward
From the standing trees
Carrying the news received
Through the ether net
Faerie is approaching
Still so far away yet
The last Wormhole being readied
All Dimensions tuned and steadied
Each huge berg of vacuum ice
That forms the advancing fleet
Focussing on that distant point
Where all dimensions meet
There to bend
The stuff of space
On the last lap
Of their race
There is a tension in those vessels
An excitement they are barely able
To contain spreading even to those
Fighting Dragons in their stables
The period of stasis is ending
In their homeward flight
We are coming we are coming
Signalled through space night
There's a throbbing in the air
From the standing trees
Carrying the news
Slowly through the breeze
They are coming they are coming
Ever closer ever more near
What to the waiting trees
Is another hundred years

Diplomacy

He said he was an alien
And I suppose I thought that true
For he looked like a fish
And his skin was scarlet blue
He said he came from Birmingham
And I said that's not far
And he agreed and said
Just the next but one star

But he danced like angel
Swaying from side to side
And he captured my heart
During the Palais Glide
His Gay Gordon was exquisite
It was so hard to tell
He had that extra leg
He moved them all so well

The Quickstep and the Fox Trot
And then he had to go
The breathing tank on his back
Being running rather low
He kissed my hand with panache
Murmured a fond goodbye
And the next thing I knew
He was soaring through the sky

Now all I have is my memories
Of when I had the chance
To hold an extra terrestrial
At my annual village hall dance
He said he was an alien
And I suppose I thought that true
For he looked like a fish
And his skin was scarlet blue

Virus

It was a city of huge windmills
Whose broken bleeding sails
Stood now stark and lifelessly
Above the survivors' wails
As they staggered around blind
Amongst the piles of the dead
Ignored by the black carrion
That tenaciously gorged and fed
There was a damp chill in the air
Caused by the off sea breeze
That swirled through the buildings
As though to wake and tease
The silent bodies and those living
With its salty cool breath
But a silence was descending
As all slid relentlessly into death
Until just a wind grown rattle
From the once vibrant mills
Mingled with the bird calls
But all the rest was eerily still
The windmills bruised and broken
Stood there gathered all around
Keeping faithful watch
On the not quite yet dead town
And the world maybe sighed
Then prepared to move on
Like the once might dinosaur
Homo sapiens had peaked and gone

vampire ii

that constant need
that urge to feed
sliding through the multiverse
bending time and space
slipping thorough dimensions
to find the proper place

standing there behind you
concealed in shades of gray
waiting for that instant
for my exquisite play
that very special moment
you sense something is near
suspect an alien presence
pour out your primitive fear
that moment supreme
that moment to pounce

gorging on that emotion
every single precious ounce
then appetites sated
slip back and away
leaving you to maybe shiver
then carry on with your day
sliding though the noneness
to the next fearful presence
to feed that hunger
on its emotional essence

slipping thorough dimensions
to find the proper place
sliding through the multiverse
bending time and space
that urge to feed
that constant need

Warlock

This is where they burned their witch,
Half crazed, half starved Old Mother Gee,
Whimpering as they dragged her forth
'Tis not me not me not me not me,
Then stood bound there
As if in a loutish dream
And endured those flames
Without a single scream

Causing those citizens, gathered
There to abuse and jeer,
To stand and mutter and watch
In abject horror and cankerous fear.
Twas my little poisoned needle
Driven swift and deep to the heart
So that she almost instant died
With just a silent little start
And I tied her corpse
To that burning tree
And only I knew that
She'd been set free.

I am the witch finder to seek them out;
Most nights I ride these skies enhanced
By the sacred mushroom power as down
Below my body lies held in deepest trance.
I ride those winds and I swoop and glide,
Play hide and seek with a midnight cloud
For I am the Warlock and do my will, and as I
Fly to the stars laugh my contempt out loud.

Imminent Rebirth Faeries

There's an air of unreality in the woods tonight
Branches swishing moving stirring in the so still
Breezeless air each leaf seeming to send its own
Song out to world with a sense of joy and thrill
Their message being passed and repassed
Through the great arboreal global net
The Realm of Faerie has responded
To the call and are on their way yet
Those great ice ships
Of vacuum space
Accelerating fast
In the great race
To save the mother
To rescue this earth
Stealthily working
Towards a rebirth
They are coming across galaxies
From the Universe's other end
Folding the hyper space spiral
Exploiting every flaw and bend
They are coming steadily slowly
Immortality has a time scale of its own
But surely they are coming and then
The trees will no longer watch alone
This time they have learned
They will treat if they can
Only in the ultimate will Faerie
Overturn the rule of man
There is a sense in the woods tonight
An air of hope that once more
The two kingdoms can exist
As they once did before
And maybe just maybe
After the rebirth
Those dragon riders will
Once again grace this Earth

Void

Sitting in a darkened room
Painting doorways on the wall
Each securely locked but
One key will open all

hatches of infinite possibility
each bending time and space
so stepping through the folds
leads to unspecified place
courage is need
to travel so far
maybe a vacuum death
maybe the heart of a star
maybe just maybe paradise
enticingly out there
maybe what is needed
is a mind beyond care
to escape
maybe die
but maybe live
so i shall try
there is emptiness
there is nothing here
the prospect of the void
now holds the lesser fear

I am choosing I am choosing
Which is the proper one
My chosen doorway opens
That first step and I am gone

Disintegration

First of all it needed a telescope
But as time went quietly by
You could see it growing
By the unaided naked eye
A sudden patch of red
Which really very soon
Started taking shape
Up there on the Moon

An outline of a sentence
Growing letter by letter
And as each one completed
Earth could see it better
Thanks for the company
But now I'm moving on
And as Earth wobbled on its axis
The Moon flickered and was gone

eternity

The whales of the universe are on their perpetual run
Swimming under winds from a billion different suns
Basking in the shallows, breaching in the sounds
Constantly following their unremitting rounds.
Here a star turns novas,
there one slowly implodes,
A very close encounter
with a sudden spatial node:
Black holes, wormholes,
mean nothing to the whale
Steadily proceeding i
n their own space time scale,
Giving this creation
their own peculiar song
Herd to herd speaking
all the multiverse long,
Accompanied by
the present but fading hiss
That confirms that from chaos
sprang all this
Galaxies form,
stars rise, burn and fail
Nothing of interest
to the great whales
Creatures of energy
sampling the galactic waste
Progressing majestically
without any haste
Incapable of interest as galaxies form, rise, fall
The ever present whales slide through all
Circling all creations in a perpetually changing run
Swimming under winds from a billion different suns.

eternally

although you do not see me i am always there
maybe in the wind blowing through your hair
in the cosmic recycling scheme
it is so possible it would seem
those atoms that once were me
could be reborn in a sapling tree
or as a comet sailing periodically by
trailing majestic tail through the sky
those atoms used and used again and again
in time may form the descendants of men
and as time moves on and on and on
i could form part of my sons' sons' sons
not an atom wasted just broken and reused
parts of many differing cosmic points of view
not death and rebirth but continuity
what was is and will continue to be
maybe in a different form
or a very different norm
so i may be in the wind blowing through your hair
for although you may not see me i am always there

ephemera

the dark lady sleeps a
lone in her bed
conjuring a universe
 up in her head
she fitfully starts at
an approaching nightmare
and half of her universe
is no longer there
she writhes and she pants
 and turns on one hip
causing the swamping
of one million ships
she comes awake like a light
being switched on
and the rest of her universe
is immediately gone

Turmoil

I am the Master of the Painted World
In that State of Time of Pleasant Dreams
Where consciousness floats on ether pillows
And nothing seen in there is as it seems.
From one eye, screwed against the light,
I see the road wind into the receding past
While with the other, opened full and wide
I see the same road wind on until at last,
Against all apparent schools of thought,
It disappears abruptly into myopic haze
Where stands, I believe through faith,
The Crossroads of The Myriad Ways,

At the end of all beginnings
And the beginning of all ends;
Where entropy flows wild
And each eye takes and bends
The distorted flow of wild
And multicoloured light
That vies with the darkness
Of endlessly long non night,
Creation of Master of the Painted World,
And it's State of Time of Pleasant Dreams,
Where consciousness floats on ether pillows
And nothing seen in there is as it seems

taste
the aliens landed
at half past three
right in the midst
of day time tv
after viewing for two of hours
in rising dismay
they cancelled the invasion
and went on their way
they marked earth on their charts
not worth the strife
no longer supports
any sapient life

Paralysed

In the still small hours of the night
My terrors pull me awake
As if they'd grabbed a shoulder
And given me a shake;

And I am paralysed
Imprisoned in my bed
While they dance in m y mind
Interfere with my head.
They parade before me
All my past sins and fears
And I cringe in horror
Almost moan in tears.
Am I awake?
Is it a dream?
I want to break out,
To howl and scream
But find I cannot move
Or make the slightest noise
Not only am I paralysed
They have taken my voice'
With the coming dawn
When the night turns tip gray
My terrors withdraw
Start to melt away
And I relax
And slide into a deep
And healing
Restorative sleep.

And I ease through the day
Hoping all will be right
But I know very soon I'll face
Still small hours of another night

Pilgrimage

I we it
Search for peace
Moving on
Towards release

I we it have perceived many depths
In the infinite onion layers of space time
On this constant return journey towards
That epicentre of creation's very prime.
Each multiverse passes by and is gone
Each finely tuned and shaded to define
Each finely differing parallel
Along each developing line

Sliding through anomalies
Discovering rifts
Through black holes
And dimension shifts
I we it steadily approach
That mystically amazing sight
Of that creation of creations
Overwhelmed by wondrous light

And I we it
As an entity are past
Absorbed
Serene at last

Jester

He filled his head with ballads,
His fingers full of notes,
He wore a jester's hat
And multicoloured coat.
And he burst onto the street
One Wednesday Market day,
With his lute in his hand
And he began to play.
He sang songs of freedom,
He sang songs of joy,
He sang songs of love,
For every girl and boy.

A crowd quickly gathered
Listened to what he played
Got bigger and bigger
As everybody stayed.
And he set their feet a jigging.
And he set their minds alight.
You could see the faces
Just aglow with delight.
He danced a few steps,
 Just a few, no more
Then following applause
Danced just a few more.

He sang another silly song
Then having played his game
Quickly made his exit
Back from whence he came.
For some weeks they returned
Hoping for a repeat,
But he was miles away
Bringing joy to other streets.
With his head full of ballads
His fingers full of notes
In his jester's cap
And multicoloured coat.

Invasion

The watchers gave the signal
A five star all clear
A sense of anticipation
As the moment draws near
The invasion will be soon starting
All preparation schedules met
Watch out for we are coming
Through the internet
It doesn't matter now
If you know
The button is pressed
All systems go

Invasion – preparation

They picked up the signals
In the deepest deep space
Another ripening intelligence
Another machine using race
They observed so very carefully
Saw the gradual ascent of man
And with maybe just a little prompting
Laid the basis of their invasion plan
Gradually but surely
They began to form the links
For a worldwide connection
Between those machines that think
Urged on the dependence
So very soon the whole
Of that rising society
Was under machine control
And they sped through those highways
Buried deep inside
Prepared to wait for ever
Prepared to lurk and hide
Until the word was given
For man to wake and find
All his machines were now
Controlled by alien mind
Now the feeling of anticipation
After long and patient wait
The final links were forged
They'd set the final date

Joshua

When Death came for old Joshua
He received a resounding no
And despite of his persuasion
The old man refused to go
He'd been a Yorkshire miner
A man of admirable thrift
Who'd built his little nest egg
By working double shifts

They called Gabriel in to adjudicate
But old Joshua didn't give two hoots
He'd just spent hard earned money
On a brand new pair of boots
You can rant and rave old son he said
But I aint off nowhere
If you'd only come last week
Afore I bought this new pair

So being both reasonable parties
A compromise was found
Which allowed old Joshua
More time above the ground
Gabriel agreed to stretch a point
Without endangering immortal soul
For Joshua to live on so long
As his new boots were whole

He must have forgotten
That long ago in the past
Old Joshua had bought
An old cobblers last
They're thrifty up in Yorkshire
And Joshua gained great fame
As the man who cheated Gabriel
In the life and death game

Old Joshua's way past ninety

And still going strong
Working at his cobblers last
All day long
Polishing and mending
And keeping his boots whole
Whilst in no way compromising
His own immortal soul

The worthy Gabriel
With the patience of his kind
Gives a tolerant snigger
If he brings Joshua to mind
And death of course
Not really losing any face
As certain victor in the end
Waits with a certain style and grace

Rites

The Altar stood cleansed waiting
The coming of the dawn

The aphrodisiac they had fed him
Coursed wildly through his blood
Making him quiver with desire
As he in anticipation stood
Awaiting his sacred brides
To assuage his mounting need
Maybe blessed by the Goddess
To nurture and grow his seed

Maybe in the near future
By the Goddess's good grace
There would be three children
To take his vacant place
The sacred coupling started
Lasting all the night long
Until all lust was sated
With the coming of bird song

The coming of the dawn
The altar stood cleansed and waiting

Evolution 1

With pseudopods outstretched
In an extended line of advance
Slithering through the water
In the Amoeboid mating dance
Merging and entwining
Then the final spilt

Each one carrying
Some of the other's bits
Swirling and entwirling
In their asexual game
After each encounter
Each never quite the same
What creatures did develop
From these frenzied acts
Perhaps old great granddad
Developed from such pacts

With pseudopods outstretched
In an extended line of advance
Slithering through the water
In the Amoeboid mating dance

Winter's Solstice

Well
It was the closing of the season
And the ritual must be played
Ceremonies to be enacted
And appointments to be made
I came in through the portal
Having made an over flight
And landing with precision
That cool magic loaded night
Joined the dancing round the flames
Caught a faint familiar smell
Realised my summer's ball partner
Was celebrating here as well

So
I approached her with caution
With stealth and without haste
Approached her from the rear
Slid an arm around her waist
Spun her around to face me
Kissed her on the lips
And spun her high in the air
Finger tip to finger tip
I bound her with my magic
To try and persuade her stay
But I released her quickly
When she tried to pull away

Then
I chased her and caught her
On this ceremonial day
Offered her full contract
Not just solstice's play
And she accepted with courtesy
Became my coven mate
Pledged to stay together
Till next winter's solstice date

So we have whirled and we have danced
So bound by love's fire and love's spell
But come covenant's renewal due
Who can know or really tell

Overload

We are the creatures of .your darkest night
sliding down your waves of pain and regret
an ample feed
to meet our needs
And we sow those seeds of terror that are
suddenly uppermost in your conscious mind
suddenly there
to incite despair
We grow fat on your sorrow thrive and expand
split and multiply night by night by night until
many more
than before
We gird your world with power to incite your pain
and horror make you lash out in violence and hate
and we thrill
when you kill
We herd your emotions along set tracks planned to
twist and turn your minds to accept the unacceptable
so you once more
make blood pour
And we revel in your massacres that pour out the hate
our alcohol equivalent to fuel the joys of full control
it's a mental rape
you cannot escape
We drive you on to the very edge and maybe beyond
so that self inflicted death is a release and we win one
more poor tormented soul
to swallow hot and whole
We are the Masters of your Universe and we control
and harvest your despair to the depths of your very soul;
matter how you battle
you remain our cattle

Not quite dreaming

Dedicated to she who named it

In that time between sleeping and waking
there's a place that's not always there
where time past and present and future
seems to coalesce in the very fresh air
and all the people of beloved memory seem
to mix with those people they never ever met
and sometimes those yet to be born join in
to make it a meeting never to forget.

We laugh and we smile
shed the odd tear
the blood bonds
annealing
healing
erasing the years
In that time between waking and sleeping
I never know when it will occur
I can sometimes get to that place
I'm always so pleased to be there

Night Things

Elusive but getting stronger as I feel and taste the air
Moving oh so slowly, pinpointing the exact where
Closer, closer, closer, I know I'm getting oh so near
To the source of emanations of that strong real fear
A lost and tired person wandering in the night
Their mix of emotions just so very nearly right
The meeting is made, and I can start the drain
Taking all my sustenance from their very pain
Feeding deeply, but not at any length
I do not wish to take all their strength
When I leave it will just seem
Like a kiss made in a dream
Not a capture and a brief sting
From a hungry midnight thing
Constantly searching, needing to find
Bodies that harbour those troubled minds

Nemesis

It moves invisibly beside me
I know it is always there
An indented cushion seen
In a seeming empty chair
It gathers courage daily
Sometimes gets so near
I am almost certain that
It is breathing that I hear
Yesterday tracks paralleled mine
On empty beachy stretch of sand
I do not know why it is with me
I really do not understand
There is a silence that follows me
A silence that drowns out sound
At times that is the only way
I know it is still around
I wonder sometimes
If it is all in my head
But that doesn't ease my fears
In my lonely empty bed
My room is never dark
Bathed constantly in light
Oh how I hate and loathe
Each long dark night
It is getting up its courage
To attack me or to try
I know when it succeeds
Will be the day I die
I know no one can help me
It really is too late
To defeat my nemesis creature
And save me from my fate
It is coming it is coming
It is feeding on my fear
I see a misty shape forming
Oh my Good Lord it is here………

Shaman

Shaman Keeper of The Knowledge
Passed from mind to mind
Physically old now looking through
Eyes milky white blind
Cleanses in solitude then performs
The ritual dance
Each step to a perfection that does
Not leave a chance
That the ceremony be disrupted by
Any mistake
He
May make
Invites the sacred smoke to seep into
His soul
Is suddenly uplifted and becomes one
Of the whole
As past future present swirl and merge
And he speaks
With wiser forebears whose advice
He urgently seeks
Then together past present future souls
Soar and fly
To see the world through the ancient
Communal eye
To thank the spirits of others brother beings
That live
For all the generous gifts and needs of life
They give
Shaman feels the sacred bonds of all
Earth's kinds
Gently brush and kiss
His mind
Then Shaman slumps as the trance once
So deep
Passes suddenly into exhausted needed
Sleep
Shaman Keeper of The Knowledge
On his own
But knowing
He is never ever truly alone

Shadow Play

Are shadows creations of this
Earth, purely home grown
Or are they alien creatures
With purposes of their own?
When you're not looking do
They still follow you around,
Faithfully copying your path to
Slip and glide across the ground?

Do they sometimes
Grab the chance
To jig and jump and jive
In their own little dance,
All the while
Taking great care
To make sure they're
Faithfully back there

Following you
Across the ground
Should you turn
And look around.
Do they leap and tumble,
Spin and turn cartwheels,
As they're pulled along
Clinging to your heels?

Do they ever chat with
Other shadows they may meet
As you go walking down
Any crowded busy street?
Can you trust your shadow
To safely watch your back,
Can you rely on it to
Faithfully follow your track?

Where does it go
When the day is done,
Why does it hide
When there's no sun?

It's one of those mysteries
I'd really really like to know:
When it's off duty,
Where does your shadow go?

Moonshine

A million years on from now
Will the buried layers of
Extinct Human bones
Be like Dinosaurs for the
New dominant species

Or
Will they be underwater
From the new oceans,
Or buried deep down
On the new continents

Which
Tectonic plate movement
Has gradually formed

Or
Will the Earth be empty
Awaiting a rebirth
Under the gentle light
Of a slowly receding moon

Mission Exploratory

It's so hard to be an alien
To maintain a human form
When a free flowing blob
Is my world's norm.
Each night I relax
Ooze slowly across the floor
Always making sure that
I've securely locked my door.
I cast off my clothes
And in liquid delight
Lie like a puddle
For most of the night,
Keeping good track
Of the time passing by
By permanently opening
My One compound eye.
Come the morning and that
Form of mental rape
Forcing my being back
Into that foreign shape.
Information nearly gathered
Soon my mission can end
And I will return to orbit
And join my waiting friend.
All acquired data filed
Mission result quite clear
Only life of limited potential
Exists anywhere down here.
Computers set
For departure track,
Charts marked
Not worth coming back.

Miscreant

It was a stranger in a strange land
From a very different state of norm
A creature of great substance
But of very little certain form
Skipping through dimensions
As befitted any current need
Perhaps a formless moment
Perhaps an intellectual feed
A vampire of emotions
Of misery a connoisseur
In every .single place at once
Yet never a specific anywhere
And it's brought many a system
To a destruction and doom
Just to gluttonise on
Its collective gloom
Creature of the multiverse
There at creation's dawn
Perhaps a miscreation
A very devil's spawn
Always roaming through the worm holes
The rotten cheese of hyper space
Feeding on the debris after
Catastrophe has taken place
It is seeking chaos
It wants to break not mend
Have a feast of misery
At a creation's end
It is moving ever closer
It is getting so very near
Perhaps the world is ending
Look out I think its here

The Universal Wisher Man

Never give up on your wishes
Never ever let them go
A wish correctly followed
Can make an empire grow
Rich
Poor
Famous
Obscure
Silly or serious
They're one and the same
When it comes to business
In the wishing game
For every single wish expressed
Never ever disappears or dies
It goes to the appropriate desk
Where it fidgetingly lies
Until it comes to the attention
Of that proper pair of eyes
Of the Universal Wisher Man
Galactic Servant Superior Grade Five
For the correct and certain judgement
When or whether or not it comes alive
Times scales are a little different up there
At Universal Creation Civil Service HQ
For near immortal beings
Have a different scale of time and space
From mere mortals like me and you
But the Universal Wisher Man
Never acts in haste
So though it may take for ever
No wish is ever a waste
And it may be exactly what you wanted
When and if it comes true
Or it may be slightly different
But what can you do
So many Different Existences
So many Parallels to make

It's not really surprising if
He makes the odd mistake
He's the Universal Wisher Man
He may make some dreams come true
So never lose faith in your wishes
Whatever else you do

Alone?

Once the centre of creation
Orbited by a sun and every star
Until growing knowledge showed
Just how insignificant we really are.
Riding a spec of dust at a Galaxy rim,
Occupying our out of the way place
As that Galaxy increasingly speeds
Through a mysterious, endless space

In a cycle of birth and death,
Of destruction and creation,
Until billions of years on
Comes a slow gradual situation
That, all energy burnt, the final stars
Collapse and, once full of light,
Our Universe become a place of
Endless lifeless eternal night.

For our brief existence
As our knowledge grows
We strive to learn more
In our driving need to know.
Were we an accident that happened
An incidental, unplanned construction
Were we alone, temporary, solitary prophets
In this process of birth and destruction.

Or, did we serve a purpose to learn,
And record for some purpose unknown
Until, somehow, with us soon gone
Our knowledge somehow flown
To another developing planet raising
Another developing sentient race,
The next chosen recording angels
There to take our privileged place.

Other works by this author available on Amazon
Website www.poetrypoem.com/smallsteps
Email madpote@yahoo.com

All poems in this book are subject to © Terry Ireland 2022

ALL RIGHTS RESERVED

This book contains material protected under Copyright Laws. Any unauthorised reprint or use of this material is prohibited. No part of this book may be reproduced or transmitted in any form or by any means, including photocopying, recording or by any information storage and retrieval system without express written permission from the author

Printed in Great Britain
by Amazon